Everywhere

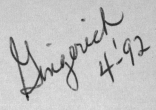

BRUCE BROOKS
Everywhere

SCHOLASTIC INC.
New York Toronto London Auckland Sydney

ISBN 0-590-45163-4

12 11 10 9 8 7 6 5 4 3 2 1   2 3 4 5 6/9

Printed in the U.S.A.   28

First Scholastic printing, January 1992

For my dad, and his

Everywhere

One

I was sitting in the backyard, in the shade of the roses, but I heard them step onto the sidewalk way up the street. The sidewalk along my grandfather's street was a single, long slab of dimpled concrete. Sidewalks were a pretty new idea in this part of Richmond, and that is how they built them; when someone stepped on it at any point, the steps vibrated along the whole block with a kind of clack and boom. My grandfather said many times he was going to take a big chisel and a small sledge and cut through in five or six places, to kill the vibration and allow the sidewalk to shift when the ground froze, so the whole thing would not crack and crumble. But he did not do it, and now it was probably too late. During the night my grandfather had suffered a heart attack.

At least that is how my grandmother put it: "Poppa has suffered a heart attack." She was quite a proper person, but she had never said anything so *book*-proper before. I had the impression that there was nothing else you could do with a heart attack, verbally, but "suffer" it— you couldn't "undergo" it or "encounter" it or any of the other words adults use when they want to avoid saying something has power over you.

At ten, I had no idea exactly what a heart attack was. I had heard "attack" used in such a fashion only in regard to kinds of food—my mother often had a "pickle attack"—or baseball. People had all kinds of attacks during baseball games, as I well know. My grandfather and I spent five nights a week beside his radio on the screened porch, listening to games played all over the country by the Yankees, broadcast from faraway New York, where my grandfather had grown up, and picked up by a huge antenna he had erected. In these games a player sometimes had a "wildness attack" or an "error attack," causing my grandfather much concern.

I was trying to be concerned now in exactly the same way. I tried to fret and frown the way he did while waiting to see if a wild pitcher would get a strike over on a 2–1 count. From my grandmother's seriousness I gathered the situation demanded such tension. A heart attack was clearly more like an error attack—that is, mysterious and difficult to overcome—than a pickle attack, which could be solved by a trip to the store.

The feet coming down the street numbered four. My grandfather had taught me how to listen to the steps and count the feet. Two would belong to Lucy Pettibone, who was a kind of nurse. The remaining two would belong to her nephew, who was coming along to be a kind of playmate for me.

This morning my grandmother had told me she would be unable to do anything for me today, even to make my breakfast. I was on my own. This was okay with me. I made myself a breakfast of toast sprinkled with powdered hot chocolate, several spiced peaches in heavy syrup, and a slab of Gouda cheese. My grandfather always had a cheese with red wax around it somewhere in the house. He drove an ambulance in Belgium and Holland in World War I, and developed a taste for such cheeses then. As a rule I found them too sharp, but I enjoyed chewing the wax he peeled from his slices. He allowed me to do this in spite of my grandmother's protests that red dye was poisonous (she once told me that if I ate the red crayon in my box of Crayolas, I would die). This morning, however, I ate the cheese and left the wax unchewed.

Later my grandmother came downstairs to tell me she had telephoned for Lucy Pettibone. Lucy was taking care of her nephew and could not leave him, so my grandmother had invited him along too. "It will be good for you to have someone to play with," she said. I thanked her, but I didn't mean it. I played just fine by myself. And I wanted to fret about my grandfather. When the Yankees were in trouble, a person didn't go play somewhere—he hung by the radio, leaning and tight. I couldn't hang by the bottom of the stairs, because my grandmother asked me to stay outside. But I could at least sit tensely in the shade of the roses.

My grandfather liked the roses better than anything but the Yankees and me. He had created three new kinds of rose, all by himself. When you do that, he said, you get to choose a name for the new kind. The one that was peach-colored with red splotches on it he named *Arlena* for my grandmother. The one that was white with dark red edges on the petals he named *Phyllis* for my mother—not for my father, who was his son, but for my mom. One that was small and yellow, the best rose I had ever seen, the only one that looked like you wouldn't break it if you breathed on it, he named *Peanuts*—for me. I was sitting beneath this bush now.

Presently Lucy came puffing around the side of the screened porch. She knew better than to go to the front door—not because my grandmother didn't allow black people to use the front door, but rather because *nobody* used it except strangers. Lucy was no stranger to anyone in this part of town. Up until a couple of years ago, she had cleaned nearly everyone's home once a week. Then, for a summer, she had stopped housecleaning and disappeared. When she showed up again in the fall, it was in a white dress and cap and shoes, without which she now never appeared in public. She had mysteriously become a nurse over the summer, completing studies begun long ago at the University of Virginia. The people in our neighborhood were getting old; they were not sickly, but certain failings had begun to show up. Before long, Lucy was working most of the houses pretty much the same way she had as a housemaid, except, I believe, for much higher wages.

"There's the boy," Lucy huffed to someone, pointing at me without greeting. "He does love to sit in strange places. I found him once in the clothes hamper. Been there the whole time I scoured the tub and sink *and* floor, sitting in with a week's dirty pajamas and towels and the like, without making a peep. You be nice and don't beat him up, now."

Lucy had stopped and was looking behind her, where someone was evidently hiding. This was no great feat—not nearly as clever a concealment as my stint in the clothes hamper, for example. It was no great feat because Lucy was large enough to obscure any *three* children, even, say, with one of them riding a tricycle and the other two holding balloons. She weighed nearly three hundred pounds, and her white uniform emphasized her expanse.

"What you hiding for?" Lucy said.

"I *ain't* hiding," a voice said. It reached me somewhat muffled by the body of Lucy between us, but I could hear plainly that it expressed annoyance.

"What do you call it, then?"

"I'm enjoying the shade back here. You cast a powerful big shade, Aunt Lucy."

Lucy, who was swift and precise despite her size, spun and grunted and jerked; suddenly a boy in blue jeans and a T-shirt jackknifed into view and landed on the lawn in a sprawl. He sat up with a scramble and looked nervously back at Lucy. She was puffing toward the back door, through with him. He sank back on his elbows and laughed. It was a fun laugh. He turned his head toward me. His face was the color of the dust on a pine trunk beneath the bark—a rich, rusty brown—and the smile was still on it. In a pleasant voice he said, "I reckon you the boy whose granddaddy's gonna die. How are you, my name is Dooley and I'm eleven."

"I'm fine, thank you," I said. "And my grandfather isn't going to die."

Dooley nodded and looked back at the house. "Well, *probably* he will. See, it's Saturday. Aunt Lucy canceled her *beauty* appointment. She don't *never* do that excepting she's needed to comfort the dead. God knows she needs the beauty treatment, as you can see."

I frowned. "Why does she bother comforting the dead? I mean—they're *dead*."

"How you think you *feel* when you dead? Pretty bad, I reckon—near as low as you can get. Think about it. No more breathing fresh air. No more eating salted cashews. No more sweating. You like to sweat? I do."

"Not especially," I said.

"No, I reckon not," he said, looking up at the rose bushes above my head. "That's why you sitting hunched up under that flower's excuse for shade while I'm out here profiting by the sunlight." He sniffed the air. It was thick with the scent of the roses. "You a sissy?"

"No."

Dooley nodded. "I didn't think so, really. I'd smell them roses a lot too, if I lived here. Well," he said, pushing up to his feet, "I reckon we best do something. I'm supposed to take your mind off your troubles while my aunt soothes the dead upstairs."

"They're more my *grandfather's* troubles," I stipulated. "And he's not dead. But okay. What do you want to do?"

He shrugged. "I like to do most anything. You got any maraschino cherries?"

"No," I said. "If we did, I would have eaten them for breakfast."

"Then you *do* know what's good," said Dooley. He looked around the yard. There was nothing much to see except rosebushes and a dogwood and a magnolia and a pine. "Well," he said. "Unless your idea of a good time is cutting down a few trees, I don't see where we got much choice."

I was puzzled. "Much choice?"

.

He looked at me. "I reckon we ought to go about saving your granddaddy. It's interesting, at least. And ain't nought else to do."

I stood up, careful not to knock the blossoms with my head. "What do you mean—saving my granddaddy?"

Dooley glanced up at the dormer windows on the second floor of the house. "Which one is your granddaddy's?"

I pointed to it. He stared, then looked at the back of the house from side to side. "I could climb up that porch awning and grab ahold of the rainpipe and look in there," he said. "But you could save me the trouble. What animal does your granddaddy favor?"

"Oh," I said. "He likes dogs a lot."

Dooley shook his head impatiently. "I don't mean what he likes. I mean what he *favors*. What animal he *looks* like."

"Oh," I said, "*favor*." I thought for a moment. "He's got very thick hair. Sometimes he messes it up so it stands out from his head and then he roars and chases me around the dining room. When he does this he looks a lot like a lion."

Dooley looked at me in a strange way. "Why

does he chase you around the dining room?"

"It's usually when we've been waiting and dinner is a little late. He says he's hungry and since his she-lion isn't bringing him any dinner he has no choice but to commence eating whatever is at hand."

Dooley still looked a bit perplexed. "But he don't eat you."

"Not really," I said.

Dooley shook his head. "Well, a lion ain't gonna do us much good. I mean, we won't likely run into too many lions out here. Anything else he look like? A squirrel, maybe?"

I thought. "No."

"A mole? Does he blink much?"

"No. He has very good eyesight. He used to play minor-league baseball."

"Maybe some kind of bird. Birds are tough, but they better than lions. I can bring down a starling or a grackle with a rock. He look anything like a grackle?"

"I wouldn't say so. I'm sorry. I guess he just looks like my grandfather to me."

"Then I best take a look," he said. And before I could say anything he trotted softly over to the porch, pulled himself up onto the tin awning above the stoop, grabbed the rainpipe, and slung himself up under the dormer. He looked down at me while pointing to the window, moving his mouth to say *This one?* I nodded. He waited for a while, then edged his head up sideways until, I guessed, his right eye cleared the windowsill. He ducked down and seemed to think for a minute, then took another peek, and came down.

"How does he look?" I said. Dooley glanced at me and looked away. I grabbed his wrist. "Is he all right?"

"Well, he ain't dead. But—well, he don't look much like a lion."

I dropped his arm. Dooley said nothing. I asked, "What *does* he look like?"

Dooley took a breath. "A turtle. Man look an awful lot like a box turtle at this time."

"A *turtle?*" I said loudly, my voice cracking on the word. "What do you mean, a turtle? That—that's not an animal. That's a *reptile*! They got cold blood! How could you say my grandfather looks like a reptile?"

Dooley was wincing at my hollering, and put

his hands up. "Take it easy, man. I don't mean no harm. He's probably a handsome dude when he ain't just had a heart attack. But he *did*. And he don't look so—so *warm-blooded* right now."

I shivered. "Is a heart attack bad?" I said.

"Bad enough to make a lion look like a turtle, I reckon." He waited a moment, then added quietly, "Aunt Lucy says ain't nothing you can do when they have a heart attack except watch 'em turn blue and call the mortuary."

"Is he blue?"

"No, man." Dooley patted my shoulder. "He ain't blue by a long shot. He just looks a little tiny bit like a turtle, is all. His head's kind of squinched into his neck and his face looks a little bony and his eyes got that look a turtle gets, like they don't really see much going on around them on account of they're about to get pulled inside a dark shell for a while. Don't worry. He be roaring and chasing you around the living room in no time."

"Dining room," I said. I had a terrible vision of my grandfather, encumbered by a huge spotted shell, moving on those groping flat legs, knocking over furniture as he slowly moved toward me in a chase, his beak opening and closing, but no roar coming out.

"Sure, sorry, dining room. But listen—the point is, now we can save him."

"We can? By knowing that he looks like a turtle?"

"That's the ticket," he said. Then, leaning a little closer to me, he added, "It's called *the soul switch.*"

"Did you learn it from Lucy?" I asked, hoping against all instinct that despite the stirring title it was a legitimate medical strategy.

"No," he said. "But it's the kind of thing my Aunt Lucy gets from her spooky uncle down in Newport News."

"I'd rather use something she learned from one of her nursing teachers at the university in Charlottesville."

Dooley laughed. "Shoot," he said. "She ain't been in any nurse university. She ain't even been in Charlottesville except on the bus passing through. She says she don't need to learn a new way of tricking people into feeling good; she can already do it just fine on the cheap. She says she

16

saving the money for *me* to go one day and be a doctor if I want. I just might. Besides," he said, giving me a keener glance, "they don't *let* coloreds into that place yet. Aunt Lucy says they *going* to in five years at the most, but not now. Doesn't your family even know *that*?"

I frowned at all we were apparently missing, but came back to what we believed: "But she *said* she finished up her studies down there last summer and became a nurse."

"Shoot. Only thing she finished up was a boy-friend named Jojo who was a no-account and sucked her money dry for July and August," Dooley said. "She found out he wasn't going to marry her at the end of the summer and gave him catfish poison. I reckon he's still in the hos-pital in Newport News. Can't no doctor figure out what's wrong with him so they say he had a stroke."

"Is he fat?"

"No," said Dooley. "Aunt Lucy knows better than to take up with a fat man. She says they don't feed you."

"What is catfish poison?"

He sighed patiently. "Well, you know how

catfish are. They get old and smart and just hunker down on the bottom of the river eating trash and tearing up tree roots and never getting caught. You can't hook them. They *eat* hooks. You can't trick them. They smarter than most white people."

"Why do you want them?" I asked.

He looked at me first as if I were crazy, and then as if he felt sorry for me. "I guess you never had king-cat steak, pan fried in pork fat and pepper."

"No," I said. "I've never had that. Is it as good as maraschino cherries?"

He smiled. "Near about. But it's a whole lot harder to get. Can't go to no store and buy a king cat in a bottle. Only way to get one is with poison."

"Do you pour it in the water?"

"No. That dilutes it before it sinks, so it barely stuns the cat, though sometimes you get a medium-size snapping turtle to float up, and he's almost as good. No, you roll the poison in balls of white bread dough and put a marble inside for heft, so the thing will sink too fast for the cats to eat it. It dissolves in the water down where they at, and they kind of get it oozed into them. Then you lay back in the grass and wait, because if you got the right side of the river you going to see a king cat float up inside an hour."

"Dead?"

"No. Just real sleepy and a little swole up. The poison don't hurt them near as much as it hurt Jojo. They can't move much, but they still breathing."

"Fish don't actually *breathe*," I corrected him gently. "It's more that they have this system for extracting the oxygen—"

"My, you *do* pick, don't you? Well, your grandpappy ain't going to breathe no more than a fish if we don't get cracking after some turtle. There a creek near here?" He stood tall and scanned the edges of the yard.

Without thinking I pointed out the back gate. "Through there, down the alley, and west into the woods there's one. Why is it that we need to look for turtles?"

He started toward the gate. "Told you. The soul switch."

As we walked across the yard I asked, "Where did you learn about this . . . switch thing?"

"Comic book," he said over his shoulder. "Indians out west use it all the time when a brave gets shot. *Always* works."

"Oh," I said. This was better. A comic book, to me, was almost as good a source as the University of Virginia, and I had long revered Indians as the highest of people—smart, private, secure in their distance from everything *I* knew. I followed him out the gate and down the alley. It was paved with crushed coke, which crunched beneath our sneakers. When we reached the edge of the field past the old dairy building, I touched him on the elbow and angled off across it. He followed. He started whistling at one point, but broke off; I believe it was because he suddenly remembered the somberness of the occasion, and did not want to mock the grieving of someone whose grandfather was so low that he was required to undergo something as desperate as the soul switch.

Pretty soon we came to some persimmon trees, and I cut through them to the path I had made myself over the previous four or five summers, and we wound downward through denser woods that started to thicken with cedars and pines. "Well," said Dooley, panting slightly, "you do know your way around *here*." He seemed to be implying that there were a good many places I did *not* know my way about, though the only place we had been together was my grandfather's yard and I certainly knew that place. I didn't think much on this, though, because in a moment we had arrived at the sudden slope of mica-dotted sand that led to the creek.

"Here we are," I said quietly.

Dooley nodded. We stood there a minute. It was a small creek, maybe six feet across, with a shallow middle and pools as deep as three feet near the bank, where the sandy bottom had washed away as large rocks or tree roots created silent, swift currents beneath the surface. The sun barely reached the surface of the creek, stippling it with pale spots like spring snow on a bush. The place smelled like sap and waterlife. I sniffed deeply.

"You like it here," said Dooley. I nodded. "Me too," he added. I nodded again. We stood for a few minutes more. Then he said, "Your grandfather show you this place?"

"No," I said. "I found it myself."

Dooley whistled. "You *do* hide. You ever bring him here? He ever been right on this spot?"

I shook my head, and fought a stab of anguish. I had *meant* to bring my grandfather here, many times. Many times we had been sitting in his "chaise lounge" in the backyard watching fireflies and drinking iced tea at sunset, and there was a quick half hour of twilight left after we finished the crossword puzzle in the newspaper, and I would want to spring up, grab his hand, and lead him out the back gate without a word. He would have come. He would have come with me without asking a single question. That's the thing. But I never did it. I saved the place for myself. Saved it even from *him*. Why? So that I could give away the secret to this stranger?

I felt something on my shoulders and flinched, thinking it might be a snake dropped from the cottonwoods. Too late I realized it was Dooley's arm, which he removed at my jerk. *Oh, no*, I thought—*he'll think it's because he's a Negro and it isn't and* . . . I burst out crying and buried my head in his T-shirt. He put his arm back over my shoulders. It *did* feel light and cool as a water moccasin.

"You strung pretty tight," he said.

I groaned, and managed to say, "I just wish I'd brought him, even once. He would have liked it, he—"

"Well, you can thank your stars you didn't. Or *his* stars."

I sputtered for another few seconds, but as usual my curiosity about a point of logical analysis dragged me back from the lunging of my heart. "Why? What do you mean?"

"Well," he explained patiently, patting me on the shoulder and gently letting me go, "if he'd've been here, he'd've *captured* it. When a man gets to a certain spot and it strikes his fancy, he takes it on into his soul, see. It becomes *his*. And all the critters in that spot become his right along too. You can't leave them out, even if they ain't visible at the time. So it stands to reason you can't do the soul switch with them."

"How do you know this place would have struck my grandfather's fancy?"

He spat discreetly into the creek, arching a

neat sparkle of saliva into the water like an experimental probe. Somehow it wasn't vulgar; it seemed more like an homage. "Only a fool wouldn't like this place," he said, "which I'm assuming your granddaddy ain't."

As ever, I pressed. "Why?"

"Because Lucy wouldn't cancel her beauty for no fool."

We looked at the water. I thought about my grandfather, and Lucy. What was she doing up in his bedroom? If we were out here messing around with vague voodoo, was she up there really getting down to it, slinging chicken blood and moaning spells? The real doctor had come in the morning, and left. I hadn't thought about why my grandmother had then called Lucy; it had seemed a natural thing. But what did Lucy actually *do*? I had a horrible fear, for which I felt guilty, that Lucy, because she felt most useful "comforting the dead," was secretly nudging my grandfather toward that condition in order to be at her best. I was haunted by the apparent ease with which she administered catfish poison.

All of a sudden I surfaced from my deep frets:

Something had happened in our little creekside patch of ground. I widened my eyes and watched. Nothing had moved—the creek slipped by as sleekly as before, the sunlight speckled everything quietly, the mica in the sand glinted. Had I heard something? No; at least, I heard nothing now. Had Dooley done anything? No; we were still standing still, me with my hands slanted into the front pockets of my khaki shorts, Dooley with his stuck like spatulas into the back pockets of his jeans.

Yet I sensed there was a difference in Dooley. Close beside me his body was nearly humming with alertness and tension. I glanced sideways at his face, moving my head as little as possible. He flicked his eyes at mine urgently, and then back at something ahead of us. I followed his line of sight. I saw something moving in the dead leaves in the shadow of a rock. Dooley clicked his tongue, and the movement stopped; then with a sharp rustle the animal dashed up the bank and vanished into the woods. I almost screamed—I had been expecting a turtle, and the creature's speed had made me feel as if the laws of nature had suddenly changed. But it was not a turtle. "Little coon," said Dooley. "Little *tiny* one."

I let my heart pound down to a steady beat. We stood. Minutes passed in silence. Dooley was content with it, but I wasn't. I needed something to know. So, finally, I took a deep breath and asked my dreadful question: "How exactly does the soul switch work?"

Dooley didn't look at me; he was scanning the bank. "Every person has a kind of animal they got their soul mixed up with way back when the world was made. You can tell by what they look like. And what happens is, if you can catch one of those animals when the person is fixing to die, and you bring it to the right spot near the person, and you sing a little tune, then—well, you switch them."

"Switch them?"

He nodded. "Trade off the animal for the person."

It hit me. "You *kill* the animal?"

The rise in my voice made him look at me. "Sure," he said, with a little challenge. "Sure you do. What's so bad about that?"

"You want to kill a turtle in my grandfather's name? That's cruel. That's vicious. That's . . . it's . . . it's *death*."

He stared at me. "Right," he finally said. "For the *turtle*."

I wanted to run back to the house. I wanted Dooley and Lucy to go away. "Let's go, then," I said. "I've never seen a turtle around here."

Dooley continued to watch me for a moment. I think he might have given in, if he hadn't heard something. But he did. He snapped his eyes back to the bank across the creek and crouched. There was a kind of *skritch* coming from a sunny rock hidden from us by a low-hanging tree branch. Through the leaves I could see a small dark shape moving—slowly—across the bright rock.

"Let's *go*," I said, pulling Dooley's arm.

But Dooley shook me off. His eyes looked smart and eager, and he tensed his legs by bending slightly. Then he took off, springing silently over the creek in a scary leap that seemed to last and last, with his arms up and out, his legs tucked in a graceful splay, his neck bent forward and his head darting. He landed with a small *whump*, and before I could even turn away he had flicked his arm at the rock, peered at something in his hand, and uttered a satisfied cry. I stood; I couldn't move. Dooley stood too, and held his arm out to me. I saw the black, lacquer legs digging at the air; I saw the head bobbing and pointing; I saw the filtered sunlight catch a tiny speck of moisture in the face that strained toward me in the air above the creek: It was a yellow eye, and a moment later the light picked at the other one. The head stopped bobbing. The turtle looked at me. There was no doubt, none whatsoever, that it had a soul.

Two

We took our prey back through the woods and
alley—or, rather, Dooley took it, while I blazed
straight ahead, with my eyes down, crunching
saplings, poison ivy, and finally coke underfoot.

Dooley did not offer to let me carry the thing,
and I did not offer to take it. Generally, I *liked*
holding animals. I found them all the time—
moles in the rose mulch, woolly mice in the
garage, green snakes in the summer grass, chip-
munks in tree stumps, a flying squirrel that
dropped down our chimney and landed with a

puff in the ashes of the fireplace, and lots of raccoons. One evening I took the trash from the kitchen to the metal can out on the edge of the alley and found the lid on upside down. When I lifted it and peered inside, I met the hopeful gaze of a large coon who must have flipped the lid instead of dislodging it as he examined the can's interior the night before. He seemed to be in no hurry to leave; after a moment I realized it was because he knew I was bringing new garbage. I lowered the can onto its side, but he wouldn't come out until I placed the remains of a dinner roll ten paces from the can's opening, in a slash of moonlight. The coon trotted over, plucked the roll from the silvery grass, and left.

"Hey," said Dooley, catching up with me. I half glanced his way; he was holding the turtle low on the side away from me. "Hey, what's the matter about this turtle? You scared of it?"

"No," I said.

"You acting like it's the Creature from the Back of the Lagoon. You never touched animals before?"

"All the time," I said.

"But you ain't *killed* any before."

"I've killed snakes. Lots of them. One time I found a nest of baby copperheads and shoveled them onto a piece of slate in the garden and chopped them up."

Dooley made a dismissing gesture with both hands. The turtle swung into view briefly and I was shocked to see it had no head or legs—for an instant I thought Dooley had prematurely slaughtered it, and I was angry. But of course turtles do that. It's their gift.

"Ain't no big thing killing baby copperheads," he said. "They don't have the poison to kill a kitten."

"Actually, they have *plenty*," I said. It was easy, as usual, to talk about details that didn't seem to matter. "And they can be even more dangerous than adults. The adults bite you and squeeze out just the amount of poison they think you need; they *pace* it, see, and sometimes they might hold back and you might live long enough after the bite to get help. But the young ones don't know about pacing. They get their little fangs into you and they let fly with everything they've got. No holding back. You can die faster with a baby sometimes than with an adult."

" 'Sometimes'? How you gonna compare? Dying *once* is mostly going to wrap up the Copperhead Speed Test at the halfway point." He laughed.

I sagged a bit. Dooley cut his chuckling short. He tried to rally me.

"How come you know so much about copperheads?"

"I read some books."

Dooley shook his head. "Snakes bad enough hiding in the grass, without you have to go reading about them when you're nice and snug in bed at night. You know anything about *nice* animals?"

We were back at the rear gate. I stopped, watching the house. Nothing moved. Somehow this seemed ominous, as if I expected a dormer to shift slightly in greeting, or the chimney to sway with a tiny wave, or the walls to expand and contract in breaths. Usually a house reflects signs of life right back at us. But not now: This house was as still as a collection of right angles could be.

"What about nice animals?" Dooley repeated, putting his arm around my shoulders.

"Bats," I forced myself to say. "I used to catch bats."

"Now *there's* a cheerful critter to bring up," he said, laughing again. I smiled. "Man's creeped out by a nice box turtle while his granddaddy's fading, but he wants to talk about *bats*." He spread his arms, hunched his neck, and made a fangy voice. "Blood!" he whispered. "Blood! Anybody fixing to die around here?"

I found myself laughing too. "No, really," I said. "Bats are really neat."

He was spinning through the gate, wings high, hands crooked like a witch's, with the turtle held aloft in one claw like a poisoned apple. "Neat!" he cackled. "I'm *neat*! And can't nobody catch me, 'cause I'm *fast and blind*!"

"I can catch them," I said, following him. "Listen. Really, I know how. I figured it out. This June I caught eighty-eight of them."

He stopped spinning and looked at me. "You lie like a rug."

I shook my head firmly. "I have it all written down in a notebook. You see," I said, lifting my chin a notch, "it was a scientific experiment."

"Sure," he said. "Just like Lucy's a nurse."

I sighed slightly and took a tolerant tone with him. "Look. I read in a Mark Trail comic about how bats have radar. They beep out these sound waves and the waves bounce back at them off of objects, and they catch them, the waves I mean, in their antennae the way we catch light rays in our eyeballs. And the bats get an idea of the things around them, the shapes and the motion and everything. They eat bugs, so when something flies by them they sense it and zip over to check it out, and if it's a bug they snap it up. Well, all I did was fake them out by throwing a little rubber ball up in the air when they flew by. They'd think it was a moth or something and follow it nearly to the ground, and I'd whip a blanket over them."

"That's science?" he said.

I shrugged. "Near enough."

"Any of them die?"

I shrugged again. "I tried to keep a few in a box at first. Six of them. They died."

"So tell me then," he said, "how come you so spooked about saving your grandfather's life with a scientific experiment on this here turtle, when you already snuffed six bats and wasn't *nobody* in danger?"

I stammered, and stopped, and thought. He didn't give me long. "That's right. Now you see we can't be worrying about anything, because we're *scientists*. Your granddaddy's depending on us—he *needs* some science. And right about now what we need is a mesa." He looked around as if he thought maybe he'd overlooked a mountain somewhere in the yard.

"A mesa? Then we don't need to be in the house?" I quickened with relief, and realized one reason I had resisted the soul switch was my fear that we had to kill the turtle close by my grandfather.

"Shoot no. Got to do it in a different place. Give the souls a chance to fly by each other in the sky. That's how it always is in the Indian comics—they do the thing in the desert on a mesa or a butte or something, and the souls whiz through the dark and bingo, the dude takes the spirit of his animal brother and hops to it." He kept peering. "Do you know what a butte actually *looks* like?"

"I think it's a huge hill with a flat top," I said. "The closest one is probably in Colorado."

"Oh," he said, brightening. "Then maybe that garage will do." He started toward the small, old door in the stucco side wall.

"No. Not in there."

He checked for a moment, looking at me, then took two more steps. "Why the flip *not*?"

I said nothing. But I knew I could not go in the garage while my grandfather was in a precarious condition—the garage, more than the screened porch with its radio or the *Peanuts* rose with its shade, would surround me with signs of all I stood to lose with him.

The garage was where my grandfather took me to make things. I remembered clearly the first time he had brought me there, perhaps six years before. My grandmother had found me in the kitchen pounding nails through the bottoms of her copper saucepans. She screamed and cuffed me on the top of my head and cried hard, but when my grandfather came he sat down next to me and gently took the hammer. "What are you trying to make?" he asked, looking me in the eyes calmly.

"Bells," I told him.

"Ah," he said, nodding.

"They have things inside that make them go," I said.

"Yes, they do," he said, and I saw he was pleased. My grandmother wailed above us like a storm that rumbles but cannot strike. He was *pleased*. "How do you know this about bells?"

"Santa Claus let me ring his."

He turned to my grandmother with a grin. "The Salvation Army. At Thalhimer's. Remember? I didn't even see him looking inside the thing. Can you believe it?" He turned to me. "What do you want the bells for?"

"I just want to *make* some."

"Why?"

I thought. He watched me. I said, "Because I know how."

"Right," he said. He hoisted me up, kissed me, kissed my grandmother, who by now was silent. "We'll buy some more pots," he said. "Right now we're going to go make some bells." And he took me out to the garage and we made them.

And the next week we made jewelry, necklaces for my mother and grandmother out of brightly colored transistors and resistors whose ends I soldered together with huge glops I thought were finer than pearls. After that it was a pair of cuff links for my dad, made from pieces of copper I painted with turquoise enamel and baked in a small kiln. Then it was a yoyo from discs of wood we cut on a jigsaw, routed, augered, glued, and branded with my initials; then a brass candlestick on the turning lathe, and about ten pairs of dice from a hunk of stained ivory. And on, and on, and on—we made anything I could imagine. There was nothing we could not do there. The old door in the stucco opened into all possibilities.

I stood for a moment and let my senses remember, smelling the sharp spice of sawdust, the acrid musk of melted solder, seeing the glinting corkscrews of brass spinning from the lathe blade and the violent whiteness showing through the cracks around the kiln door, hearing the sneer of the jigsaw, the chug of the paint sprayer. I could not go there now, and I told Dooley so.

"Well," he said, "fine. I can do it myself. You can be the lookout."

"Lookout?"

"Sure. Somebody got to sneak up there by the window and spy so we know the right moment to do the switch. You do that, and I be the one do the messy work in here. I'll stand in the door, and you signal me, and . . ." He snapped his fingers. The sound was like bone breaking.

"I have to watch"—I took a deep breath—"my grandfather die?"

"No, man," Dooley said softly, giving the turtle a little shake. "You have to watch him come back to life." And with that he opened the door and went into the workshop.

I turned and sat down, facing the house.

A few minutes later, Dooley came and sat beside me. For a few minutes neither of us spoke. Finally, I said, "Are we ready?"

"Near about," he said. "Just a few important details we got to take care of." He looked at me. "What's your grandfather's favorite thing to wear?"

I thought for only a second. "Bow ties," I said.

Dooley nodded as if this made sense. "All right then. You got to tiptoe on inside there and get us one of those bow ties."

"I'm not supposed to go inside," I said meekly.

"And I ain't supposed to be out here sawing the heads off turtles to save some white boy's grandfather what he's too much of a twerp to fight for," he snapped, glaring at me. "I ain't here to do nothing but maybe tell you a couple jokes or maybe chuck the ball a little bit and *supposed* to leave you with your grieving if that don't do the trick." He jabbed me with his finger. "Boy, you want to try the soul switch or not? You got a better idea? If not, I'll tell you what I need: I need one of them ties, and I need two colors of nail polish, and if you pass by the fridge I could also use a cold drink. You got it?"

I had it. I got up, and without being aware of my steps, I passed into the angular back doorway. The only thing I dimly noticed was that the house still did not make a move to welcome me.

Three

My grandfather kept his ties in a tall cherrywood chifforobe that had a room pretty much to itself around the corner from his bedroom, on the second floor of the house. He called the chifforobe "Jeeves," after a character in some books he liked; he said he couldn't get dressed without Jeeves, and it was true. Jeeves held his four or five suits in a tall compartment for hangers, his shirts and socks in smoothly worn drawers, and his jewelry in a built-in bird's-eye maple box lined with spruce-green felt. But the chifforobe's best feature was a collapsible nickel tie rack that folded out from the inside of its left-hand door, to offer my grandfather his fabulous array of silk bow ties.

There was a photograph in my father's wallet of my grandfather and me when I was three months old. I am sitting naked on the large porcelain sink top in the second-story bathroom, facing into the mirror above it, grinning toothlessly; behind me is my grandfather, with his head on a level with mine, also smiling into the mirror; and around my neck is a perfectly knotted paisley bow tie. My grandfather holds each jaunty end between thumb and forefinger, as if he has just finished tightening it from behind. Between my feet is a Leica camera, which my grandfather somehow managed to trigger so that our reflection is caught. It is proof: I *always* loved his bow ties.

He would wear no other kind of tie, and neither would I. On dressy occasions, while my father cursed over his Windsor knots in the bathroom and my mother and grandmother fussed with scarves and jewelry and powder, my grandfather and I stood cool before Jeeves. We drew on shirts (crisp and fragrant with starch), trousers, socks, and suspenders, and laid our jackets on the single chair with which Jeeves shared the room. Then my grandfather would lightly rake the hanging curtain of bow ties with his hand, sending their pointed and squared ends hopping in a dance of colors and patterns. "Well?" he would say, "which one for me?" I would study his shirt (he liked bold stripes) and his suit fabric (he was fond of checks, houndstooths, pincords, and herringbones), and take several ties to hold against his waist, where shirt met suit. Finally, I would choose one and hold it up to him, and he would thank me and knot it without a moment's hesitation. Then he'd invite me to choose one for myself, which he tied while I stood on the chair's ottoman and watched in the small silver-framed mirror above the tie rack.

Never once did my grandfather second guess my choice of a tie for him. Never did he raise an eyebrow or laugh when I chose, say, a violet-and-burnt-orange paisley to go with a shell-pink shirt and a licorice-stripe seersucker suit; or a red-and-black box pattern for a forest-green tattersall shirt and a chestnut jacket. Many times, in the beginning, my grandmother would gasp when she saw him and say, "Ellington, you *must* change that tie!" but he would only smile, kiss her cheek, and, winking at me, give the tie an extra tweak. "It's the very tie for this splendid evening, my dear. Shall we go?"

And now, as I climbed the stairs at Dooley's bidding, what would be the very tie for this terrible day?

The house was as quiet as a building without people; I had to keep reminding myself that three other persons were indeed inside, and I mustn't disturb them. It helped me, to focus on that number: three, three, three. All *alive*. Not just the bulbous lively Lucy, the nervous lively grandmother, but also, if we were not too late, the faintly warm-blooded, faintly lively grandfather. Three, three, three.

At the top of the stairs I paused. The landing was strangely dark. The door to my grandparents' bedroom was shut. I realized I had never seen it so. The three windows in the back of this room always let light out onto the landing. I wanted to open it, just for the light. Even some light that had passed nearby my grandfather would have been better than this silent stillness in which he was hidden.

But I did not open the door. I turned the corner, and went into his dressing room.

Jeeves stood tall and red, burnished by the afternoon sun that was slanting in the small window, the color of the wood glowing beneath the clear old varnish. I stood for a moment with one hand on the chifforobe's flank; it was warm, curved, more nearly alive than the house, and it relaxed me. I took a deep breath, and smelled wool, naphtha, and a peppery wood smell. I knew opening Jeeves would be much like going into the garage. I considered closing my eyes, creaking the door open a few inches, and snaking a blind hand around to yank a random bow tie off the rack, but I knew I couldn't snatch and run. Dooley's words were with me: *This is science.* I had to do this exactly. The right tie was called for. I opened Jeeves.

In my resolve, I must have yanked harder than usual. The tie rack unfurled and the ties kicked up their ends at me like the legs of a spider surprised in a private dance. I jumped back, hit my calves against the ottoman, and toppled; flailing a hand to catch something, I grabbed the wad of ties and pulled them cleanly off the rack and onto my chest as I landed in the chair.

I looked. The ties lay on me like a hundred shredded Halloween costumes, twists of grass green and ice blue and fog gray and fire red. I panted. The ties clung to my white T-shirt, rising and falling as if they were some kind of beautiful new leech matching my breath. I did not move.

I wondered if my fall had made noise; I listened, but no one came from the bedroom. I watched the ties as my breath calmed. How could I choose? How could I get out from under them?

After several minutes, I realized something was in my right hand. I held it up to see. Threaded around my middle finger was a tie of polished indigo silk specked with tiny, pale-orange triangles outlined by single threads of luminous aqua. It was, I suddenly felt, the most splendid thing I had ever seen. I stood up, letting the other ties slide off me, and I walked out of the room.

There was something else. What was it? I

paused on the landing, and remembered: nail polish. Two colors of nail polish. I went into the bathroom, pulled open drawers until I found the right one, and from the pointed bottles selected a deep crimson and a fleshy tan. Then, without thinking, I looked into the mirror.

This was the mirror that had shown the camera that goofy baby smile; now it showed me only a dull-looking face with gloomy shadows around the eyes and beneath the cheekbones. Was it *me*? I stared. There was no deep recognition. The face staring back, the torso in the white shirt, the hands holding bottles and tie— I knew them, of course, but try as I might I could not see that they contained and defined my self. My self was whizzing around somewhere, *everywhere*, and would not come in for a landing. In this one moment it hung in the shadowed silence of the cool sand and the creek bed, it moved with the hovering dust stirred by the open door of the garage, it exuded the dense scent of the darkest rose in the garden. My self fretted with Dooley as I dawdled. It matched my grandmother's flickering worry. And— yes!—my grandfather's cool, fleeing heartbeat, quiet and distant like a stream going underground. Three, three, three. *But where was I?*

I remembered feeling the same way once before, when my grandfather, my father, and I were sitting on the back lawn one fall evening as night crept up on us. We had been out there for an hour, and I kept lifting my hands every couple of minutes, holding them up and studying them as the loss of twilight made them less and less distinct. As their outline faded, I felt myself escaping into the night breeze, lifting beyond my blinking eyes and damp feet, and I was filled with a certainty about the world, and the sky—that things were moving everywhere, and things were at the same time still; and that I, too, would not be bound by a movement of my body, or a moment of knowing a fact, or a sudden burst of laughter, or a dream, or a long night's dark sleep. I was filled with bliss. Tears came to my eyes and I noticed through the blue air that my grandfather was watching me. I wanted to tell him. Without thinking I whispered, "I'm everywhere." He seemed to nod, and he whispered back so softly I wasn't certain

I heard his words or just knew them inside: "I'm there with you."

A noise sounded from downstairs, in the kitchen, and my attention came back to the mirror. As I focused on the face I noticed tears once more filling the eyes; but looking further, I saw the bow tie knotted neatly around my throat, and my hands holding the ends in a jaunty gesture, as if they had just tied it.

Another noise clanked from the kitchen. I recognized it: the rattle of the ice trays as the freezer was closed. I stepped silently across the landing and took the steps two at a time without making a sound, as I did every Saturday morning on my way to listen to early radio serials. I turned to the right and stopped at the kitchen door, just in time to see Dooley plucking a small green bottle of ginger ale from the lower part of the refrigerator. He turned toward me, saw me with a start, and stopped.

"Hey," he said, forcing a smile. "Hey, man. How'd you tie that tie?"

"My grandfather taught me," I said. "What are you doing in here?"

"Getting a drink," he said, waggling the bottle. "There's an opener in the garage. Let's go have a sip and get going. Did you get the stuff?" His eyes dropped to my hand.

"What were you doing in the freezer?"

"Nothing, man, just looking for ice. Come on, let's get." He hustled me around and out the door to the backyard, where the shadows of the garage and the huge magnolia were turning the grass cool. I let him take the polish and unscrew the lids and smell it, making a squinched face as he did so. He tightened the lids again, stuck the bottles in his front pocket, and glanced at my tie.

"Now we all set," he said uncertainly.

I pulled one end of the tie and it came undone, then I slipped it off and handed it to him. He took it with relief. He was excited, but there was something going on I couldn't figure out. But then, I couldn't figure out the soul switch, or for that matter a heart attack either.

"Here's what we do," he said, nodding, looking back over his shoulder at the garage door, up over my shoulder at the window, quickly into my eyes and quickly away. "We got to paint some sacred marks on the turtle's back. I figure your grandfather's initials will do, and a couple squiggles and stuff. The Indians always do this to the animal. Like a sign to the soul that's going to be racing around looking for a place to go. Then we put a piece of something belonged to the man around the animal. Then you climb the roof, and watch, and—"

"You do the painting and the thing with the tie," I said.

"All right, sure, sure," he said, looking at me closely with a stab of concern. "You feeling peaked or anything? You need some g.a.?" He held out the bottle.

"I'm fine," I said. "My grandfather's initials are EDB."

"EDB. Yeah. All right." He looked up at the window, and let out a big breath. "Well, this is the part where the Indians always get real holy, and they don't talk. You sure you don't want to come in and do the turtle with me?"

I shook my head. He nodded, and surprised me by stepping forward and taking me in a sudden tight hug. I felt the ginger-ale bottle cold against my back, and something even colder through his shirt, but before I could think about it the hug was over and he was sneaking across the lawn like an Indian scout in a cowboy movie. I turned back toward the house.

A few minutes later, I heard him whisper from the door: "All set now." I nodded without turning, and went to the rose trellis beside the porch.

I had never climbed onto the roof. The thought of doing so had never occurred to me. But when Dooley had done it earlier, I had watched in surprise at his easy technique, and I found now that following his steps led me up just as easily, despite my internal resistance to the idea. From the top of the trellis I grasped the gutter, careful not to hang my full weight from it, and supported a kind of lunge that brought my chest against the hot slate shingles of the roof. Pressing my chest and cheek and hands against them, I pulled from the waist and curled my legs under me. Then I rose to a kneeling position, and crawled slowly over to the middle dormer.

Beneath the sill I crouched to catch my breath, but noticed that I didn't really need to; in fact,

I was very calm. I looked down at the yard with mild curiosity, noticing that the rosebushes were planted in two parallel S-lines, a pattern I had never appreciated from ground level. I glanced into the magnolia tree that still towered above me, and saw, in the crook between a seedpod and a leaf, the rubber knife I had lost weeks before while throwing it at tall, imaginary pirates. Then I heard a voice from beyond the window, and I leaned up and looked in.

The first thing I saw was Lucy. She was just hauling herself up hastily from the armchair next to my grandmother's vanity, with a look of concern on her face. To her left, my grandmother was wriggling, with an odd shoulder motion, to emerge from the corner of the room, into which she had sagged standing up. She, too, had a sharp, piercing look. I followed her eyes out and saw my grandfather.

He was in his bed with the head against the side wall to my left, and the foot in the middle of the room, closer to me. I could not see his face. The reason was that his legs, beneath a pale-blue sheet, were jerking in quick little kicks, blocking my view. I stood up, slipping for a second as a shingle scrabbled loose and clanked over the gutter and into the yard, and held on to the windowsill, craning to see past his thrashing legs. But they kicked higher now. My grandmother was grabbing at them helplessly, her face full of fear; Lucy, frowning, was leaning over my grandfather's torso and seemed to be striking him with both hands in the chest.

It was frantic. I pushed my hands against the window; I couldn't even touch the *air* in there. Wildly, I waved my arms and looked around as if for help. I heard a sound from behind me, and in an instant I turned and recognized it—the jigsaw starting up in the garage. A dark shape jumped into the doorway and vanished, and too late I realized it was Dooley, who had heard the noise, who had turned on the saw, who had seen me waving my arms from the window, and who was now going to kill something.

"*No!*" I screamed. But the whine of the saw suddenly veered into a shriek that meant it was cutting something hard. I looked back in the window; Lucy's sweating face had turned toward me quickly, but she was back at her pounding. "*No! Don't do it*," I screamed. My voice was clear and unrestricted—there was no limit to its volume and space, and I used it: *"No! No! No! Don't don't don't!"* over and over until the window in front of me flew open, my grandmother's thin arms grabbed mine and jerked me in one motion over the sill and to my knees on the floor. I was going to holler again but I looked up first.

There, on the bed, I saw my grandfather, his legs flat, his hands clenching the crisp pleats across Lucy's bosom, his back lifted and his head peering at me. Yes, I thought, yes he *does* look like a turtle, his nose sharp and skin dull as plastic, his moist eyes seeking, his mouth opening and closing. "Don't," I said, a last time. And as I watched, the mouth closed, and the eyes blinked, and dried. The skin seemed to soften a little, catching the fine pink light from the setting sun; the nose lost a bit of its edge. The hands in the starched cotton relaxed, and the eyes focused, on me.

I met them, and I said, "Don't go everywhere."

My grandfather looked at me as if I had just given him a very good idea. His mouth opened, and in a whisper said: "Okay. Sure. I won't."

Then, with a shaky wink, he lowered himself back and closed his eyes. Lucy pulled a burgundy blanket over his chest, and before she put me out of the room I got to see it going up a little, and down a little, up, and down, easy as music.

Four

For the next hour I don't think I did a thing but stand a few steps outside the back door, where Lucy left me, facing the yard and the garage and the alley. I wasn't in shock, I wasn't elated, I wasn't even drained—I was just feeling kind of quiet, so I stood, with my hands in my pockets. I remember things happening around me: my grandmother calling the doctor from the phone in the kitchen, and weeping with what I finally recognized as relief; a mockingbird singing from a stake in the garden; Lucy agreeing reluctantly to help make some soup, and leaving to go back upstairs in a huff when she and my grandmother got into a stupid fight about a chicken neck missing from a stewing bird in the freezer; a breeze stirring the roses and scattering scent my way; the doctor arriving, and greeting Lucy with great respect; and, finally, Lucy fetching Dooley with offhanded crossness, ignoring me except for a tap on the head, and tromping away with her nephew in tow. I listened to them clack and boom down the sidewalk all the way to the end of the street.

Most of all, though, I remember Dooley emerging from the door of the garage, looking sheepish but brave. He watched me stand there for a long moment.

"Is the dude alive?" he asked, in a thin voice.

"Yes."

He exhaled a big breath. Then he looked to both sides, and over my shoulder at the house. His eyes sought mine, and when I met them he looked down at his hands. So did I.

The light skin of his palms was smeared. Cupped in them he held a dark object the size of a jacks ball. "The bone broke the saw blade," he said, "but I got the head off clean." He said this softly, respectfully; the tone was so reassuring that for a few moments I didn't bother to figure out what he was showing me, or why. When I realized, he had left to take the thing somewhere out in the alley. I heard him crunching over the coke going away, then crunching back. He came close to me. His hands were clean.

"It worked," he said. His eyes were brilliant, strange with some knowledge, and it wasn't just the sunset light; they were so bright it seemed as if they must hurt.

"Was it bad?" I said.

"No!" he said. "No, man! Easy. Flip on the saw, take the signal—"

"Okay," I said.

He poked me on the shoulder, and smiled. "You got your granddaddy back. You got him back, your grandma's crying for joy, Lucy's the genius nurse, I'm the big chief medicine man. Everybody's happy, right?"

I don't know why I said it: "Except the turtle."

The light in Dooley's eyes dipped, and he looked to the side. "Well," he said, "one of them was going to die this afternoon anyway, you know? Listen, I'm going to go clean up that saw." And he went back into the garage, and stayed, coming out again only when Lucy called for him so they could go.

But these things, which seemed to be happening around someone else, did not stick or connect in my memory. I went to bed early that night, and the next day marked the start of my grandfather's recuperation. He called it "re-coop," and complained that it was just like shut-ting in a chicken that had got out of the roost and lit off toward the forest.

"My troubles were over," he would say. "And somebody had to go and drag me back. Think of it: No more cauliflower. No more shaving. No more Republicans. I was headed for the Big-time, and now I'm back here where the humidity is ninety-eight percent and the Yankees are in fourth place."

The Yankees were indeed in fourth place, and I worried about it—no longer because I simply loved the Yankees, but now because I was afraid their error attacks and wildness attacks and blown games would push my grandfather's heart past its new, lowered limit. We listened to every single game, me sitting calmly with my glove on, trying to set an example that he ignored, as he twitched and fumed and groaned in his chair on the porch. As the summer passed, though, and his agonies failed to crush him, I worried less. And once, in an early September game just before I was to return to my parents' house and resume school, he swatted the side of the radio and said, "Turley, if you don't stop getting behind every hitter, you are going to give me a heart attack." I must have stiffened, because without missing a beat my grandfather put his arm around me and said into my ear: "But only in my baseball heart."

The Saturday before I was to go, he was fully dressed in weekend clothes and washing his breakfast dishes when I came downstairs in the morning. He fried me two eggs, spread my toast with honey butter, and carved me a Bartlett pear, topping each half with a maraschino cherry. While I ate, he said, "You're going tomorrow. Today let's make something."

I shivered. He didn't see; he was whistling and pulling an herbal tea bag from a steaming cup. I took my time, and chewed my food. Hoping that I sounded both casual and committed, I said, "Hey, why don't we go to the *pool*? You can wade and float and stuff, take it easy—the water will be good for you. Let's do that. Let's go to the pool!"

He whistled as if he hadn't heard me, then brought his tea over to the table and sat. He took a sip, and made a face, and looked down into the cup. "More than anything," he said, "even black tea, I miss making things with you."

I felt my chin start to quiver. He took another sip of tea, said, "Bah!" and got up to pour it in the sink, looking out into the backyard until I had time to settle down. I finished my breakfast. He cleared my dishes and brought two pencils and some paper, and we spent the next half hour designing a pencil box with a sliding top and a stamped metal nameplate, for me to take back to school. Then we got up, and headed out to the garage.

I had not been near the garage since the day of the heart attack. The place gave me the creeps. But now my grandfather turned the door handle, and stepped in. I followed. He sniffed deeply

and grinned: "Smells like work!" I sniffed too:
There were the familiar aromas of oil and wood
and glue and dust. He looked around, and so
did I, glancing first at the jigsaw. Its blade was
gone, but that was often the case. The rest of it
was spotless, and so was the floor.

My grandfather was inviting me to poke
around in the wood bins to select the materials
for my pencil box. I tried to concentrate, and
chose some fine pieces of thin maple plywood.
He laid out our plans and drew cut lines on the
wood. Then without a glance he fit a new blade
into the jigsaw, flipped it on, and started to cut.
Behind him I winced at the sound, and pushed
my fists into my eyes when the blade bit into
the wood with a shriek—but then, in a moment,
as the saw kept screaming, it gradually became
just the jigsaw again. My horror passed. I in-
haled deeply, and the sawdust smelled good.

"Better find the glue," my grandfather said. I
did, and put the can in a pot of water on the
hotplate. Then I turned on the router for the
grooves in which the lid would slide, just as my
grandfather handed me the side pieces. I lined
up the blade, held the first piece in place, and

lowered the spinning bit. The maple shavings twirled away like tiny party streamers, and I smelled their nutty scent. The groove was holding true, and I was absolutely focused on it— nothing else existed but the blade and the line and the wood. When I finished the first piece, flipped off the machine, raised my goggles, and ran my finger critically along the groove, I remembered all at once why I loved to lose myself in making things. I got ready to do the second groove, vaguely aware that my grandfather was saying something.

"What?" I said, lowering my goggles and reaching for the switch.

"I said, somebody's moved in while we were away. His name, it seems, is Ed."

I turned around, lifting the goggles. "What do you—"

My grandfather was holding out a scrap of plywood. There, standing on the end of it with its nose in the air, was the turtle.

I stared. "Friend of yours?" said my grandfather.

"It— What do you mean?" I stammered.

He laughed and pointed at the turtle's arched

shell. I looked: Painted across the top in large crimson letters were the initials ED. Around them was a rough circle of tan arrows.

"Yes," I said. "Yes, he's a friend."

"Well, you're lucky to find him again," he said. "He must have been trapped in here for a month. I found him over behind the scraps, completely boxed in. He must have survived on bugs and seepage at the base of the wall. Plus there's something over there that died, and he picked it clean."

I went over to where he pointed, and knew already what I would find. I looked down into a little hidden nook. There were spots of damp, and spots of waste, and spiderwebs, and in the middle, picked clean, three fourths of a chicken neck.

My grandfather had put the turtle flat onto one palm, and was lightly touching the top of its head with a finger. The turtle flinched and pulled its head partly in a few times, but then he arched his neck up and let himself be stroked.

"Where'd you find him?" asked my grandfather.

"I'll show you," I said. "Come on."

Five

Sunday I got up early, before anyone. I put on blue jeans, a gray sweatshirt, sneakers, and my Yankees cap, and snuck quietly out the back door and across the yard. I tried to keep the coke from crunching while I was near the house, but fifty yards later I ran down the alley all the way to the railroad. Then I followed the tracks east.

I wasn't certain where Dooley lived. I knew Lucy's house, because I had ridden with my grandfather several times when he used to take her home. She lived in East Holler, or Hollow, a large neighborhood of narrow, sloping streets and houses sunk into knolls. It was a low place, cool in the summer beneath vast trees that loomed above as if hung in the sky. There was a good chance Dooley lived in the Holler too.

But I wasn't going to try to find his house. Instead, I was going to look for him in the Holler churches. I knew Lucy went to church every Sunday morning, and I counted on her relations doing the same. I figured I could check for him at each church inside an hour, and if I was lucky, I'd find him.

I left the railroad tracks when the gravel banks started getting steeper as the ground dropped away. I slanted through the hickory trees and found a path that snaked down. The green shade was very cool, and the dust of leaves starting to turn made the air smell like burned cinnamon. It was September in the woods before it would be September in the streets.

After a while I smelled smoke, and walked toward it until I found a low ridge to follow. The trees thinned, and the ground cover started giving way to grass. In a few minutes I saw half a dozen chimneys ahead. I was in the Holler.

Finding the churches was easy, but staying out of sight was not: Everyone in the Holler seemed to be going to church, walking along the streets, talking and laughing, but somehow subdued in a contented way. I scuttled behind houses and kept low across fields of dying tall grass. At the first church, I climbed a little loblolly pine until I could peer in through a broken pane in a tall stained-glass window on the side wall. It was the perfect spot to spy, and I wondered if I would have such luck at any of the other churches.

I didn't have to go to any of the other churches: After I had been watching for only five minutes, Dooley walked in the front door, pushed gently from behind by a tall handsome man with a mustache. I grinned when I saw Dooley, and the grin stayed the whole time I watched. He walked with a careless dignity, as if he couldn't be bothered to turn it on all the way. He let a girl who must have been his sister into the pew before him, looked at his father for a nod, and proceeded sideways until he could sit. He crossed his arms, held his chin high, and looked up at the windows.

I looked hard at his eyes. Were they still brilliant, strange with knowledge? The things he knew—did I know them now too? All of them? Was eleven that much older than ten? I searched in his face for the look I had thought held the terrible wisdom of death, but which, perhaps, had been nothing more than kind, nervous deception. I looked hard. I found nothing but a good eleven-year-old kid, bored, bright, and— I would never forget it—smart enough to keep quiet.

I had not planned on talking to him—what he kept to himself should stay kept. But suddenly I wanted to give him something. I was aware all at once of what he had done for me, and aware too that probably I had not even thanked him. I had just watched him walk away in his aunt's shadow, thinking only of my grandfather and myself, angry—and this was *my* secret—that a turtle had saved his life instead of me. Now I had learned that it was not the turtle after all.

What could I give this kid? I thought of the pencil box, now varnished and decorated with jigsaw cutouts, and I wished I had brought it.

I felt my pockets: nothing. *Dooley,* I thought, *I want there to be something in it for you besides a secret.*

And then I noticed it. I leaned closer to the hole in the window, and smelled the perfume and sweat and heard the rustle coming through with the warm air; and I focused on Dooley's collar. There, tied like a shoestring, with looping ends, was a flash of indigo silk specked with orange triangles trimmed in aqua. Above it, he jutted his chin. His father spoke to him, and as Dooley turned his head, he gave the motion an extra flick so the tie ends slashed the air. It was splendid, it was all his—and he knew it.